Bright Lights, Big Kitty!

Read more Animal Inn books!

BOOK 1: A Furry Fiasco

BOOK 2: Treasure Hunt

BOOK 3: The Bow-wow Bus

Coming soon:

BOOK 5: Whooooo Done It?

ANIMAL INN
Bright Lights, Big Kitty!

Book 4

PAUL DUBOIS JACOBS
&
JENNIFER SWENDER

Illustrated by STEPHANIE LABERIS

ALADDIN

New York   London   Toronto   Sydney   New Delhi

ALADDIN

An imprint of Simon & Schuster Children's Publishing Division

1230 Avenue of the Americas, New York, New York 10020

First Aladdin paperback edition August 2017

Text copyright © 2017 by Simon & Schuster, Inc.

Illustrations copyright © 2017 by Stephanie Laberis

Also available in an Aladdin hardcover edition.

All rights reserved, including the right of reproduction in whole or in part in any form.

ALADDIN and related logo are registered trademarks of Simon & Schuster, Inc.

For information about special discounts for bulk purchases, please contact

Simon & Schuster Special Sales at 1-866-506-1949 or business@simonandschuster.com.

The Simon & Schuster Speakers Bureau can bring authors to your live event.

For more information or to book an event, contact the Simon & Schuster Speakers Bureau

at 1-866-248-3049 or visit our website at www.simonspeakers.com.

Cover designed by Jessica Handelman

Interior designed by Greg Stadnyk

The illustrations for this book were rendered digitally.

The text of this book was set in Bembo Std.

Manufactured in the United States of America 0617 OFF

2 4 6 8 10 9 7 5 3 1

Library of Congress Control Number 2017931083

ISBN 978-1-4814-6233-4 (hc)

ISBN 978-1-4814-6232-7 (pbk)

ISBN 978-1-4814-6234-1 (eBook)

For Helena and Mattias

PROLOGUE

Ping-ping!

Lately there's been a lot of "pinging" around here—from Mom's phone, from Dad's phone, and from the computer in the office.

Ping-ping!

Welcome to Animal Inn. My name is Shadow. I'm what you might call an escape artist. I also happen to be a cat.

No, I'm not one of those silly cats you see in videos on the Internet. That would be my little brother, Whiskers.

I prefer to stay in the shadows. That way it's easier to sneak outside without anyone noticing.

I'm part of the Tyler family. Our family includes five humans—Mom, Dad, Jake, Ethan, and Cassie—and seven animals:

- Me
- Whiskers—my little brother
- Dash—a dog
- Coco—another dog
- Leopold—a bird
- and Fuzzy and Furry—a pair of rodents (Okay, they're technically gerbils.)

We all live together in this old house in the Virginia countryside. Animal Inn is one part hotel, one part school, and one part spa. As our brochure says: *We promise to love your pet as much as you do.*

Ping-ping!

Another message?

It could be a Pekinese in need of a pedicure. A Siamese requesting a short stay. Or a llama in need of a long stay. Once, we even had a Komodo dragon bunk in our basement.

On the first floor of Animal Inn, we have the Welcome Area, the office, the classroom, the grooming room, and the party and play room.

The Welcome Area is where you'll find the all-so-important sofa. The sofa is my brother's favorite place to rest, and my favorite place to hide.

Our family lives on the second floor. This is where you'll find the kitchen, dining room, and bedrooms. You'll also find Fuzzy and Furry in their gerbiltorium in Jake and Ethan's room.

The third floor is for our smaller guests. If you need an aquarium, a terrarium, or a solarium, the third floor is for you. But if you bark, meow, neigh, or bleat, you'll be accommodated out in the barn and kennels.

Ping-ping!

Wow! Animal Inn has become so popular lately—famous even. And to think, it all started with Whiskers, a web video, and a big dog.

Let me tell you what happened. . . .

CHAPTER
1

It began like any other Saturday

morning at Animal Inn—busy!

On Saturdays, Mom teaches her Polite Puppies class. That's when a herd of little yippers invades the inn. They come to learn some manners. And trust me, they have a lot of work to do.

Dad and Jake also host the Furry Pages. That's when children read aloud to an animal buddy.

Plus, there are grooming appointments and usually a birthday party or two.

Saturday is my favorite day of the week, and not because I'm a big fan of puppies. It's my favorite day because the front door is always opening and closing, giving me plenty of chances to sneak outside.

On this particular morning, my little brother Whiskers was curled up on the sofa in the Welcome Area. Leopold was on his perch, and Dash and Coco were out for a walk with Mom and Cassie.

I was hiding behind the sofa, waiting for things to start hopping when I heard Dad, Jake, and Ethan coming down the stairs.

"I'll be outside if you need me, boys," said Dad. "I want to clear the leaves from the walkway before our first guests arrive. I can't wait to try my new leaf blower."

Dad paused before opening the front door. "I see you hiding back there, Shadow," he said with a smile. He quickly opened the door and closed it behind him.

Drat.

"Are you ready, Ethan?" asked Jake.

I peeked out to see Ethan carefully holding Dad's smartphone. "I'm ready," said Ethan. "Action!"

"Welcome to Animal Inn," Jake said to the camera. "Here at Animal Inn we promise to love your pet as much as you do. My name is Jake. Today we are going to show you Saturday chores. First on our list, we tidy up the brochures."

"Cut!" said Ethan.

"What's the problem?" asked Jake.

"It doesn't make sense to show brochures in a *web* video," said Ethan.

"Good point," said Jake. "This information is all online anyway. I'll skip that part and go straight to feeding the pets."

"Okay," said Ethan. "Action!"

"Our first morning chore is to feed the Animal Inn pets," said Jake. He walked toward the supply closet.

I slinked out from behind the sofa to see what would be for breakfast.

"Cut!" said Ethan again.

"What now?" asked Jake.

"Everybody knows we feed the pets," said Ethan. "This is supposed to be a super-cool video for our website. What's the next chore?"

"Sweeping the Welcome Area," said Jake with a sigh.

"That isn't very exciting," said Ethan.

I looked around. Ethan was right. The Welcome Area wasn't very exciting at the moment. Leopold was preening his feathers, and my little brother Whiskers was already dozing.

"Let's give it one more try," said Jake.

Ethan held up the phone. "Action!" he said.

Urrrrrrrrrr!

Just then, Dad appeared outside the window with the leaf blower strapped to his back. He wore big safety goggles and ear-protection headphones. Leaves whipped and spun all around him.

Urrrrrrrrrr!

Whiskers's eyes suddenly shot open.

He spotted the figure at the window and leaped

high into the air, paws stretched straight out in front. He soared in a perfect arc, then landed with a thump and skedaddled up the stairs.

"Wow!" said Jake, turning to the camera. "Now *that* was exciting!"

CHAPTER 2

"Did you get it?" asked Jake.

"I think I got it," said Ethan. He tapped the screen of the phone.

"Wow!" said Jake. "Whiskers can fly!"

"Check it out in slow motion," said Ethan. He tapped the small screen again.

I scurried over and jumped up on the window-sill to get a better look.

It really seemed like Whiskers was flying.

"He looks like a superhero," said Jake.

"Super Cat!" cheered Ethan.

"This could make a really cool video," said Jake, "especially if we add some background music."

"Then we can write the words 'SUPER CAT! UP, UP, AND AWAY!' across the bottom in big letters," said Ethan.

Dad came inside, closing the front door behind him. "I just love my new leaf blower," he said. "That took no time at all. How's your web video going?"

"It's going awesome," said Ethan.

"Can we upload it to the office computer?" asked Jake.

"Then post it to the Animal Inn website?" asked Ethan.

"I don't see why not," said Dad. He led the boys into the office.

I jumped down from the windowsill.

"Super Cat?" I said to Leopold. "I always thought of my brother as more of a sofa cat."

"It *was* an impressive leap," said Leopold, "with excellent form."

Whiskers cautiously tiptoed back down the stairs. "Is that scary robot gone?" he asked. "It made such an awful noise."

"That wasn't a robot," I said. "It was Dad."

"He has a new leaf blower," added Leopold.

"Well, I liked the rake much better," said Whiskers, resettling in his spot on the sofa.

"You never liked the rake," I corrected him. "Just like you don't like the broom, the dustpan, or the vacuum cleaner."

Ping-ping!

Ping-ping!

"Now what's *that* sound?" Whiskers asked. He buried his head under a sofa cushion.

Ping-ping!

"It's nothing to worry about," said Leopold. "That just means Animal Inn has received a text message."

"Forget the messages," I said. "I need to get back into position. Those impolite puppies and Furry Pages kids will be here any minute. You know where to find me."

I slipped behind the sofa, waiting for the doorbell to ring.

Ping-ping!

Ping-ping!

"Well I'm staying right here," said Whiskers. "No puppies. No pages. No problems."

Ping-ping!

Suddenly Jake and Ethan came rushing out of the office. "Whiskers!" they cheered. "Whiskers, you're a star!"

CHAPTER
3

"Who's a star?" asked Cassie.

She and Coco were just coming through the front door. Mom and Dash followed.

"Whiskers is a star," said Jake.

My little brother? A star?

I stepped out from behind the sofa. But Whiskers was right where he always was, doing what he always did. I jumped up next to him.

"What did we miss?" Mom asked, hanging up the dog leashes.

"The boys made a web video," said Dad.

"We posted it online," said Ethan.

"And it's taking off like wildfire," said Jake.

Whiskers looked at me in alarm. "Fire?" he whispered.

"It's an expression," I assured him.

Ping-ping!

"Here's a message from Sierra," said Dad, looking at his phone.

Sierra is our college intern. She's studying to be a veterinarian.

"'Love Super Cat!'" Dad read. "'LOL! Shared it with all my friends. High-five to the sofa-surfer!'"

Ping-ping!

"And here's one from Mr. C.," said Dad.

Mr. C. is Cassie's teacher. Just last week, Cassie's entire first-grade class visited Animal Inn on a field trip. It was the best field trip ever.

"'I sent the video link to the class list,'" Dad read out loud. "'I can't believe the first graders got to meet Super Cat! Up, up, and away!'"

"This is all very exciting," said Mom. "But first things first. We need to get ready for Polite Puppies and Furry Pages. Plus, Dr. Dietz, the veterinarian, is joining us today. We can catch up with the messages later."

Ping-ping!

"Hold on a second," said Dad. "This is a message from Big Dog."

"*The* Big Dog?" asked Mom.

"Yes, that Big Dog," said Dad. "It seems he wants a piece of Whiskers."

"A piece of me?" Whiskers whispered.

"Stay calm," I whispered back. "It's just another expression."

"But what would Big Dog want with Whiskers?" asked Mom.

"Not Whiskers," said Dad. "He wants Super Cat."

"This is so cool!" cheered Jake, as the Tylers made their way to the party and play room. "Super Cat is totally going viral!"

CHAPTER
4

"I'm going *what*?" exclaimed Whiskers.

"I believe Jake said you are going viral," said Leopold.

"I have a virus?" asked Whiskers. "You mean, I'm sick?"

"Good thing Dr. Dietz is coming today," said Coco.

"You don't need a doctor," I assured Whiskers. "Going *viral* means that something is wildly popular on the Internet. And right now, that wildly popular something is *you*."

"But who is this big dog?" Whiskers asked.

"Maybe it's a past guest," said Dash. "Animal Inn has hosted a lot of big dogs over the years."

"But what does the big dog want with *me*?" Whiskers asked nervously.

I looked around at all the pets. No one had an answer.

"I never thought I'd say this," I said, "but . . . Follow me to the gerbiltorium."

We all hurried upstairs to Jake and Ethan's room.

Fuzzy and Furry were having a snack in one of their clear plastic tunnels. They stopped eating and stared at Whiskers—spellbound.

"Why are you looking at me like that?" Whiskers asked.

"Can we have your autograph?" asked Fuzzy.

"We are huge fans," added Furry. "We just love Super Cat."

"Oh yeah," Whiskers said with a shrug. "That whole thing."

"Can we focus, please?" I said. "Gerbils, we have a job for you."

"Sorry, we're swamped at the moment," said Fuzzy. He went back to munching on a celery stalk.

"Totally overbooked," added Furry.

"That's a shame," I said. "But I'm sure Super Cat can find someone else for the job."

"Hold your horses!" said Fuzzy. "We'd be working with Super Cat?"

I nodded. "The one and only."

"Why didn't you say so?" added Furry. "Give us the details."

"We need you to work your magic and find a message on the office computer," I explained.

"A message about what?" asked Fuzzy.

"A big dog who wants a piece of Super Cat,"
I said.

Fuzzy and Furry gasped.

"Say no more," said Fuzzy.

"Leave it to us," added Furry.

Then they picked the lock on the gerbiltorium and disappeared into the heating vent.

CHAPTER
5

As soon as we returned to the
Welcome Area, the doorbell rang.

Ding-dong!

"I'll get it," we heard Mom call. She hurried
from the classroom to the front door.

Yip! Yip! Yap! Yap! Yap!

The Welcome Area quickly filled with puppies.

Yip! Yip! Yap! Yap! Yap!

Like I said, they were still working on being polite.

Ding-dong!

More yippers and yappers tumbled through the front door. They were followed by some of the children arriving for Furry Pages.

Usually I would take advantage of all this commotion and sneak outside. But today was different. I needed to stick around.

There were a lot of unanswered questions. Who was this big dog? And what did he want with my little brother?

Mom scooped up a puppy who was heading straight for the office. "No puppies allowed in here, sweetie," she said, closing the office door.

Good thing she didn't say no *gerbils* allowed. But now with the door closed, Fuzzy and Furry

could get to work. I sure hoped they would find
some answers.

Yip! Yip! Yap! Yap! Yap!

"Look," said a little girl, pointing to Whiskers.
"It's Super Cat!"

"Super Cat! Super Cat! Super Cat!" the children

cheered. It seemed everyone had seen the video.

With each cheer, Whiskers's confidence seemed to grow. He sat up a little straighter in his spot on the sofa and started purring proudly.

Ding-dong!

Mom opened the front door again. It was Dr. Dietz.

"Where's my Super Cat?" asked Dr. Dietz. He rushed over to the sofa and patted Whiskers on the head. Then he pulled a Kitty Krisp from the pocket of his white medical coat. "This is for you, movie star," he said.

"I guess you saw the video too, Doc," said Mom.

"Sure did," said Dr. Dietz. "I also posted a link on my clinic's website. I think our little Whiskers is going places."

"You're right about that," said Mom. "We were just contacted by Big Dog."

"Wow!" exclaimed Dr. Dietz. "Big Dog is my favorite."

Wait a second. Dr. Dietz knows this big dog too?

Mom started leading Dr. Dietz toward the classroom. I decided to follow. Maybe I could learn something. I kept to the shadows, but close enough to hear what they were saying.

"Big Dog is the biggest in the business," said Dr. Dietz.

The biggest?

"And that's a dog-eat-dog world," Mom added.

Dog eat dog?

"I actually take care of Big Dog's dogs," Dr. Dietz said.

The big dog has dogs of its own?

"And they sure are a wild bunch," he added.

Wild dogs!

Good thing Whiskers hadn't heard any of this. I was now worried enough for the both of us.

CHAPTER
6

I needed to alert the others. I

hurried over to Furry Pages.

I was expecting to find the children arranging their carpet squares while Dad and Jake passed out the books. Instead, everyone was intently listening to Ethan.

"We were just going to bring Whiskers," Ethan

explained. "But we didn't think Whiskers would go without Shadow."

"And I won't go without Coco," said Cassie.

"And why stop at one dog?" added Jake. "So Dash is coming too."

"And we can't go without Leopold," said Ethan. "He's like our family spokesman."

"So the whole Tyler family is going," said Dad.

The whole Tyler family is going where?

"But who's going to run things at the inn?" asked one of the parents.

"Dr. Dietz will lead Polite Puppies, and Mary Anne, the librarian, will be here for Furry Pages," said Dad. "Plus, our intern, Sierra, can take care of the rest of the guests while we're in the city."

The city?

None of this was making any sense.

I rushed out and nearly collided with Dash and Coco in the hallway.

"Where have you guys been?" I asked.

"Coco thought she saw Curtis in a tree outside the window," said Dash.

"Remember Curtis, the squirrel who stayed with us that time?" asked Coco. "It looked just like Curtis."

"Curtis was a red squirrel," said Dash. "This was definitely a gray squirrel."

"Never mind about the squirrel," I said. "We've got problems. I overheard Dr. Dietz talking to Mom."

"About Polite Puppies?" asked Coco.

"No," I said. "Not about puppies. They were talking about the big dog and his pack of wild dogs, who live in a world where dogs eat dogs!"

"You're not making any sense, silly," said Coco.

"I'm just telling you what I heard," I said. "And then Dad said we're all going to the city next Saturday. Why would we be going to the city?"

"Take a deep breath," Dash said to me.

"And maybe have a snack," said Coco, patting my head.

"We'll come find you after Furry Pages," said Dash.

I hurried back to the Welcome Area and looked around. Everything seemed normal. Leopold was once again preening his feathers, and my little brother Whiskers was snug on the sofa.

I put my ear to the office door and listened carefully. Were the gerbils finished yet?

Ping-ping!

Ping-ping!

"Look at this!" I heard Fuzzy squeak.

"Wow!" added Furry.

"This is big!" said Fuzzy.

"This is wild!" added Furry.

Then I heard a whir, a tear, a double thump, and a skitter.

What had those two rodents discovered?

CHAPTER
7

Yip! Yip! Yap! Yap! Yap!

The dismissal of Furry Pages and Polite Puppies was chaotic as usual. Owners were chasing after puppies. Tail-wagging puppies were chasing after one another.

Jake, Ethan, and Cassie did their best to hand out bookmarks to the children, but everyone was more interested in Whiskers. The puppies, their owners, the children, and their parents all wanted a souvenir photo.

Dash, Leopold, Coco, and I could only stare. It was pretty amazing how in only a few hours, Whiskers had gone from a regular house cat to Super Cat.

Finally, Mom and Dad waved good-bye to the last puppy.

"Time for lunch," said Mom.

"I vote for mac-and-cheese," said Jake.

"Me too!" cheered Cassie. "My favorite!"

Coco wagged her tail in excitement.

The Tylers headed upstairs. Coco started to follow.

"Psst," I whispered. "We need all paws on deck."

"But there's mac-and-cheese," said Coco.

"We need to make a plan," I insisted.

"Why do we need a plan?" Whiskers asked from the sofa.

"It's nothing to worry about, Little Brother," I said.

"Why would I be worried?" said Whiskers. "I'm Super Cat. Everyone loves me."

Just then, Fuzzy and Furry poked their heads out of the heating vent. They dragged a piece of computer paper behind them.

"Thank goodness you're finally here," I said. "What did you find out?"

"It's wild," said Fuzzy.

"And it's big," added Furry.

"I already know all about the big dog and his pack of wild dogs who live in a world where dogs eat dogs!" I blurted out.

"Eat what?" asked Whiskers.

"Cool it, cats," said Fuzzy. "Big Dog is *not* a dog."

"Not even part of the same species," added Furry.

"He's not?" I asked.

"Big Dog is a human," said Fuzzy.

"He's a TV guy," added Furry.

"TV?" said Coco.

"He has a show—*Big Dog in the Morning*," said Fuzzy.

"On channel seven," added Furry.

"It's very informative," said Fuzzy.

"We watched a clip about easy recipes for the busy family," added Furry.

"Are you saying that Big Dog wants Super Cat to be on a television show?" asked Leopold.

"Affirmative," said Fuzzy. "*Big Dog in the Morning* has a segment called Power Pets."

"And next week's Power Pet is . . . Super Cat!" added Furry.

Fuzzy and Furry pointed to the paper on the floor. Dash padded over to take a closer look.

"It says here that a private limousine will arrive bright and early Saturday morning for Super Cat and his entourage," Dash read out loud.

"A limousine for *me*?" asked Whiskers.

"This is a surprise," I said.

"Because Whiskers is going to be on TV?" asked Coco.

"No," I said, pointing to the gerbils. "Because these two actually found some useful information."

"I do hope there's fresh water in the limo," said Whiskers, licking his paw and smoothing down his fur. "Preferably natural spring water. My throat gets so dry under the bright lights. And I assume

there will be an ample supply of Kitty Krisps."

"I think your head might be starting to swell, Little Brother," I said. "What do you know about bright lights anyway?"

Suddenly we heard Jake holler from upstairs. "Where could they be?"

"I don't know," shouted Ethan. "They were in the gerbiltorium this morning."

"Let's keep looking," called Jake.

"I *am* looking," said Ethan. "And I don't see Fuzzy and Furry anywhere."

"Uh-oh, time for us to go," said Fuzzy.

"Up, up, and away!" added Furry.

They scurried into the heating vent and disappeared.

CHAPTER 8

Things were suddenly looking

up. I had stowed away in cars, trucks, and buses.

But I'd never been inside a limousine. This was

going to be exciting.

Ding-dong!

"I'll get it," called Mom, making her way

downstairs.

Surprisingly, Whiskers didn't even flinch at the

sound of the doorbell. Instead, he sat up a little straighter and groomed his fur.

"Could be a fan," he whispered.

Mom opened the front door. It was Martha, the Animal Inn groomer.

"Hi, Martha," said Mom.

"Can you believe it?" said Martha, stepping inside. "Our Whiskers is a superstar!"

Whiskers purred proudly.

"Yes, it's been quite a whirlwind," said Mom. "And next week Super Cat is going to be on TV."

"TV?" said Martha. "Then he'll need a stylist."

"Can you do it?" asked Mom.

"I can always squeeze in a VIP," said Martha. "This is going to be so much fun."

Martha gently picked Whiskers up and carried him back to the grooming room.

Ding-dong!

Mom opened the front door again. It was Monsieur Petit.

Monsieur Petit is a miniature French poodle. He has been coming to Animal Inn for his grooming appointment every Saturday since we opened.

"Bonjour," said Monsieur Petit's owner, Madame Gigi.

"Good afternoon, Madame and Monsieur," said Mom. "Martha will be with you in a minute. Monsieur can wait here, if you like."

"Très bon," said Madame Gigi. "I'll be back soon." She waved good-bye.

Ping-ping!

Mom sighed. "I bet that's more fan mail for Super Cat," she said. She hurried into the office.

"Bonjour, mes amis," Monsieur Petit said to us

with a bow. "Who is this Super Cat that Madame Tyler speaks of?"

"You don't know?" asked Dash.

"*Non,*" said Monsieur.

"Well, here he comes now," said Leopold.

Whiskers strutted out from the grooming room, looking fancy, fluffy, and proud as a peacock.

"Wait," said Monsieur Petit. "Whiskers is *le Super Cat*?"

"Hello, Monsieur," called Whiskers, prancing over to the sofa. "I suppose you've already heard that I'll be on TV next week. They're sending a limo for me and my entourage. We film in the city."

"Ooh la la," said Monsieur Petit.

"I'm looking forward to it," said Dash. "Leopold and I haven't been back to the city since we moved here."

"And maybe I'll see Curtis," said Coco. "He lives in the city too."

"Coco," I said. "Do you know how many squirrels there are in the city? You are not going to just bump into Curtis."

"I might," said Coco hopefully.

"I do miss the city sometimes," said Leopold. "There was a specialty grocer near our old apartment building with the most scrumptious dried fruits."

"Was there cheese?" asked Coco.

"Lots of cheese," said Leopold.

"There was also a lovely cheese shop in my home city of Paris," said Monsieur Petit. "Blocks of cheese, wheels of cheese, tubs of cheese. In fact, I once saw a famous movie star shopping for cheese in my little shop. She even shook my paw. *'Enchanté,'* she whispered to me. It was *super-fantastique*."

"Yes, yes," said Whiskers, admiring his own paws. "We celebrities must always remember our adoring fans."

I looked at Monsieur Petit. All we could do was shrug. Super Cat, it seemed, was getting super-full of himself by the super-second.

CHAPTER
9

Over the next week Whiskers's Internet popularity continued to grow. Along with his ego.

Usually, Whiskers and I slept on the big rocking chair in Mom and Dad's room at night. But Whiskers had kicked me off because he needed his beauty rest.

I'd been sleeping at the foot of Cassie's bed

with Coco, who for the record, talks in her sleep. Mostly about cheese.

So, on the morning of the big TV debut, I could hardly keep my eyes open.

Mom, Dad, and the kids were upstairs finishing breakfast, but we pets were already in the Welcome Area. I spotted Leopold's travel cage and Whiskers's cat carrier set out by the front door.

"That carrier looks just like my old carrier," scoffed Whiskers.

"It *is* your old carrier," I said sleepily. "What were you expecting?"

"Something larger," said Whiskers. "With plush carpeting and perhaps a sunroof."

"Oh brother," I said with a sigh.

"Yes?" asked Whiskers.

"Never mind," I said. I was starting to miss the old Whiskers.

The Tylers soon came downstairs, everyone excitedly talking a mile a minute.

Cassie clipped on Coco's leash.

Jake clipped on Dash's leash.

Mom clipped on my leash. (Yes, I have a special cat leash.)

Ethan carefully put Leopold into his travel cage.

Then Dad got ready for the real test—getting Whiskers into his cat carrier. This was not a quick or easy job. Whiskers usually went in kicking, hissing, and scratching.

But today he proudly pranced in without a peep.

"Wow," said Dad, securing the latch. "That was easier than I expected."

Ding-dong!

"That must be the limo driver," said Mom, opening the front door.

But it wasn't. It was Sierra, here to look after the Animal Inn guests for the day.

"Good morning," said Sierra, hanging up her bike helmet. "Looks like everybody's ready for the big city. Any special instructions before you go?"

"We've got two ferrets and an iguana staying on the third floor," Mom told her.

"Plus four sheep in the barn and three dogs in the kennel," added Dad.

"And please check on Fuzzy and Furry," said Jake.

"They've been a little escape-y lately," said Ethan.

"No worries," said Sierra. "What could possibly go wrong?"

Ding-dong!

"*That* must be the limo driver," said Mom, opening the door again.

But it wasn't. It was Monsieur Petit and Madame Gigi.

"We brought you fresh croissants for your trip," said Madame Gigi, handing Mom a bag from the bakery.

"*Merci, Madame,*" said Mom.

"The whole town is talking about the show," said Madame Gigi. "Now we must hurry home so we can watch Super Cat on the television."

Beep-beep!

"Whoa," said Ethan, looking out the window. "Is that for us?"

Mom opened the front door yet again. In the driveway was the longest car I had ever seen. And was it shiny! A driver wearing a fancy cap stepped out.

"I'm here for Super Cat and his guests," he called.

"That's us," said Ethan.

The limousine had two sections—one up front for the Tylers and one in the back for the pets. We all piled inside. Then Dad unclipped our leashes and shut the door.

Wow!

The limousine had plush carpeting, cozy seats, an awesome sunroof, and plenty of natural spring water.

Once we were on our way, Leopold undid the latch on his travel cage. Then he fluttered over and opened the door to Whiskers's carrier. Whiskers strode out and settled on one of the dreamy seats.

"Now this is more like it," he said.

I had to agree. These seats were even comfier than the sofa in the Welcome Area.

"I could get used to this," said Dash.

"It is very pleasant," said Leopold.

"But where are the snacks?" said Coco, sniffing around.

Just then, out of Whiskers's carrier popped Fuzzy and Furry.

"Fancy meeting you guys here," said Fuzzy.

"Small world," added Furry.

"*What* are you two doing here?" I asked.

"We've never been to the city before," said Fuzzy.

"Plus, we wouldn't miss Super Cat!" added Furry. The gerbils clapped their paws in excitement.

"Thank you," said Whiskers, taking a bow. "Thank you."

I leaned back and closed my eyes. I didn't mean to fall asleep, but the past week was catching up with me. Plus, riding in that limousine was like riding on a cloud.

CHAPTER
10

"It's Curtis!" shouted Coco.

I woke up with a start.

"Look!" said Coco, pointing out the limousine window. Her snout was covered in croissant crumbs. "It really is Curtis!"

I looked out the window as we drove. The landscape had changed while I was asleep. Instead of rolling hills and leafy treetops, I now saw crowded sidewalks and shiny skyscrapers. Horns honked. Buses beeped. We were definitely in the city.

"That is not Curtis," I said sleepily.

"I have to agree," said Dash.

"You'll discover the city is a very big place, Coco," added Leopold. "The chance of bumping into an old friend is quite small."

The limousine came to a stop. Were we there already? Was I the only one getting nervous? I suddenly felt like I had a million butterflies in my tummy.

"Places, everyone," announced Whiskers. "Places."

Fuzzy and Furry quickly scurried back into Whiskers's carrier. Whiskers followed. Leopold resettled in his travel cage.

The limousine door opened.

"We're here!" said Dad. He carefully picked

up Whiskers's carrier. "Huh. How did this come undone?" He relatched the carrier door.

"Lights, camera, action," said Jake, clipping on Dash's leash.

"You mean, lights, camera, Whiskers!" said Ethan, picking up Leopold's travel cage.

A crowd had gathered on the sidewalk outside the TV studio. They were holding signs and cheering.

"Super Cat! Super Cat! Super Cat!"

"Whiskers is famous," said Cassie, clipping on Coco's leash.

Mom attached my leash. Then she thought for a moment and picked me up in her arms. "We don't want you sneaking away today, Shadow," she said.

A man ushered us through the door and into a small room backstage.

"Hey look, they've got cheese," whispered Coco. She wandered over to a table piled high with snacks and drinks.

"This must be the greenroom," whispered Leopold.

"Why do they call it a greenroom when it's yellow?" I asked.

At that moment, a busy-looking woman rushed in. She wore black clothes and a fancy headset with a microphone attached.

"Morning, all. I'm Zoe, the producer," she said. "Glad you got here okay. Welcome to *Big Dog in the Morning*. So here's what we're going to do."

I wondered if everyone in the city talked so fast.

"You're on at ten twenty-three," Zoe continued. "We have a quick commercial to clean up from Baking Buddies. Then Big Dog introduces Power

Pets. Talks to the kids. We have Super Cat do his thing. Up, up, and away, and all that. Then you have to clear the stage pronto so we can set up for our next segment—Garden Gab. Any questions?"

"Uh, I don't think so," said Dad.

"Is that the cat?" Zoe asked, pointing to me in Mom's arms.

"No," said Mom. "This is Shadow, Super Cat's sister."

"So where's Super Cat?" asked Zoe. "You did bring Super Cat, didn't you?"

"He's in here," said Dad, holding up the carrier.

"Excellent," said Zoe. "I'll come get you in a bit."

She muttered something into her headset and quickly left the room.

"Stay close, Shadow," said Mom, setting me down on the floor.

"This is so cool," said Jake.

"I just can't believe it!" squealed Cassie.

Dad put Whiskers's carrier down and opened the door. Whiskers strutted out and shook his fur. Luckily, the greenroom had a comfy sofa. Whiskers hopped right up and started preening.

"A star is born," I whispered to Coco.

"The real star is this cheese," Coco whispered back. "Yum."

CHAPTER
11

A few minutes later a voice came over the intercom. "Power Pets, please report to the set. Power Pets, please report to the set."

Zoe popped her head in the doorway. "Follow me," she said.

"This is going to be exciting," said Dad.

"Even better than a web video," said Ethan.

We all followed Zoe down a narrow hallway.

"Super Cat goes in here," she said, pointing to a door labeled *Makeup*. "The stylist wants to do a touch-up." Dad carried Whiskers into the room.

"The rest of you can follow me to the TV studio," she said.

We entered a big open space with special lights hanging overhead. Three TV cameras stood ready in position.

"Welcome to the set for *Big Dog in the Morning*," said Zoe.

There was a small stage with a desk on one side and a sofa on the other. In the background were floor-to-ceiling windows. The Super Cat fans who had greeted us earlier watched from outside.

On the set, a helper was busy cleaning up from the previous segment—Baking Buddies. She cleared mixing bowls and cookie sheets, while a shiny, round machine hummed across the floor.

"What's that gadget with the blinking lights?" asked Ethan.

"It's our awesome robotic vacuum cleaner," said Zoe.

"We could use one of those at Animal Inn," said Mom.

"It sure would make Saturday chores more exciting," said Jake.

The helper shut off the vacuum and stowed it in a corner.

"Let's have the kids sit here and Mom here." Zoe pointed as she gave us directions. "This dog here and that dog there and the bird perch here and the black cat there and we'll put Super Cat right here closest to Big Dog."

We all shuffled and sat and rearranged until Zoe had us where she wanted us.

Dad hurried over with Whiskers, who now looked positively radiant.

"Look, Shadow," Coco whispered to me. "That is definitely Curtis." She pointed out the window with her nose, which was now covered in cheese from the greenroom.

"Sure, Coco," I murmured. "Whatever you say."

"And here comes our host," announced Zoe.

"Hi, I'm Big Dog," said a friendly looking man with a bright red bow tie. "Welcome to the show."

He shook Mom's hand and Dad's hand and waved to the rest of us before sitting down. "And this must be Super Cat," he said.

Whiskers held out his paw to be shaken. I'd

never seen him do that before. And was I the only one who heard him whisper *enchanté*?

Whiskers was as calm as could be, while I was a bundle of nerves. Had we switched personalities?

"I'll be asking you a few questions," Big Dog told everybody. "Just try to act natural. That goes for you, too, Super Cat." He reached over and gave Whiskers a gentle pat on the head.

"Quiet on the set," announced Zoe. "We're on in three, two, one. . . ." She gave Big Dog a big thumbs-up.

"Welcome back," said Big Dog. "It's time for Power Pets. Our guest today is the Internet sensation that everyone is talking about . . . Super Cat!"

I saw one of the television cameras swoop around to focus on Whiskers. Whiskers looked up and tilted his head. He stared right into the lens.

"The camera just loves him," said Big Dog. "Super Cat is a superstar."

I had to admit, everything was off to a great start.

"First, let me introduce the Tyler family," said Big Dog. "The Tylers run an amazing place called Animal Inn. Jake, why don't you tell us all about it."

Jake took a deep breath. "Well, Animal Inn is one part hotel, one part school, and one part spa. As our brochure says, *At Animal Inn, we promise to love your pet as much as you do.* And we also have lots of pets of our own."

"Ethan," said Big Dog, leaning in Ethan's direction. "How did Super Cat come to be? Tell us the whole story."

"We were making a web video about Animal

Inn," said Ethan. "And our cat Whiskers just leaped into action."

"Then Dad helped us post the video online," said Jake.

"And now Whiskers is famous!" added Cassie.

I could hear the faint murmur of chanting outside the windows.

"Super Cat! Super Cat! Super Cat!"

"Well, we'd love to see some up, up, and away!" said Big Dog.

"Oh. It's not like we trained him," said Jake.

"So he's a natural!" said Big Dog enthusiastically. "On three. Everybody help me count."

The camera people and the fans on the sidewalk and Zoe and Big Dog all began to count out loud.

"One. Two. *Three!*"

Whiskers didn't move.

He just stared at the camera. His eyes had become as big as saucers.

"Come on, Little Brother," I murmured. "You can do it."

Big Dog chuckled. "Why don't we try that again," he said. "On three. Everybody, help me count."

"One. Two. *Three!*"

No leap.

No Super Cat.

Poor Whiskers was downright frozen.

"How is this cat super?" I heard one of the camera operators whisper.

A few fans on the sidewalk lowered their signs in disappointment. Some even walked away. Whiskers continued to stare blankly into the camera.

Then he squeezed his eyes shut and buried his head under a sofa cushion.

CHAPTER
12

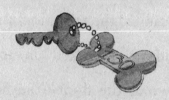

His timing wasn't great, but this

was the Whiskers I knew and loved. Unfortunately, he was in front of a live television audience, and they didn't want a timid kitty. They wanted a fearless Super Cat.

I knew Whiskers didn't want to disappoint his fans. Deep down he wanted to be Super Cat too. Who wouldn't?

I noticed Zoe nervously checking her watch. She looked at Big Dog. Big Dog nodded. Then Zoe said something into her headset.

Time was running out for my little brother to be a star. Someone had to do something to spark him into action. And that someone was me.

I quickly scanned the television studio. I looked out the windows. I looked up at the ceiling. I looked down at the floor—the floor that was super-clean.

Of course! The robotic vacuum cleaner!

Whiskers did not like vacuum cleaners. Whiskers did not like robots. It should do the trick.

I silently snuck off the set and over to the corner.

But how to turn it on?

"Come on, Super Cat," I heard Big Dog say. "Let's give it one more try."

It was now or never. In a panic, I hopped on top of the vacuum and started swatting at anything that looked like an "on" switch.

Nothing worked.

"What are you up to, Shadow?" It was Fuzzy, suddenly by my side.

"Is it cleanup time already?" added Furry.

"I need to turn this thing on," I said. "Whiskers needs my help. And fast."

"Well, your heart's in the right place," said Fuzzy.

"But your paw is not," added Furry.

They scurried beneath the vacuum.

"The 'on' switch for this model . . . ," called Fuzzy.

". . . is under here," added Furry.

Click!

Beep!

The vacuum sprang to life with me still on top of it. It turned this way and that way. I held on tight.

Whooooa! Whooooa! Whooooa!

Whiskers looked up from under the sofa cushion. He spotted the robotic vacuum cleaner zipping across the floor.

Then he leaped high into the air, paws stretched straight out in front. He soared in a perfect arc and landed with a thump. Then he skedaddled off stage.

CHAPTER
13

"Now that's what I call exciting!"

cheered Big Dog. "Let's hear it for Super Cat! Up, up, and away! And after the break, it's Garden Gab. How much compost do you really need for those tomatoes?"

"Cut to commercial," announced Zoe.

"Super Cat did not disappoint," said Big Dog. "One of the best Power Pets we've ever had."

Zoe ushered everyone off the set. The guests for Garden Gab hurried on. I took advantage of the commotion to hop off the vacuum cleaner and try to steady myself. It took me a moment to get my land-legs back.

Dad found Whiskers in the wings and settled him in his carrier. Mom and the kids got the rest of us ready to go. Then a man led us through the door and out to the curb where our limousine was waiting for us.

"Super Cat! Super Cat! Super Cat!" the crowd cheered.

Suddenly Coco pulled her leash right out of Cassie's hand and took off down the sidewalk.

"Coco!" Cassie called. "Coco, come back!"

"I'll get her," said Mom, handing my cat leash to Dad.

The rest of us got settled in the comfy limousine while we waited for Mom to fetch Coco.

Soon Coco happily piled in, all out of breath. Mom undid her leash and shut the door.

"Where did you run off to?" asked Dash.

"Smell some cheese?" I said.

"No, silly," said Coco. She settled in her seat with a big smile on her face.

Once we were on our way, Leopold unlocked the latch on his travel cage. Then he fluttered over and opened the door to Whiskers's carrier.

Whiskers stepped out and quietly settled on one of the dreamy seats. Fuzzy and Furry popped out after him.

"You were amazing, Super Cat," said Fuzzy.

"The camera really loves you," added Furry.

"Thanks," said Whiskers. He scooted closer to where I was sitting. "Uh, Shadow," he said to me.

"Yeah?" I said.

What did the superstar want now? More spring water? More Kitty Krisps? A new sofa?

But Whiskers surprised me.

"Thanks for your help, Shadow," he said. "I couldn't have done it without you."

"No problem," I said. "That's what family is for."

No matter how famous he was, Whiskers would always be my little brother.

CHAPTER
14

The ride home was pretty quiet.
We'd been up since daybreak, and we were all tuckered out.

But as we turned into the driveway, the quiet ended. A big group of cheering fans had gathered in front of Animal Inn.

The limousine came to a stop. Fuzzy and Furry quickly scurried back inside Whiskers's carrier.

Whiskers followed. Leopold resettled in his travel cage.

The limousine door opened. "We're home, Super Cat," said Dad. He carefully picked up the carrier. "Huh. How did this come undone again?" he said.

"Look at the size of this crowd," said Jake, clipping on Dash's leash.

"Super Cat is a real superstar," said Ethan, picking up Leopold's travel cage.

"Whiskers is even more famous-er than before," said Cassie, clipping on Coco's leash.

Mom leaned in next and attached my cat leash. We all started for the front door.

"There she is!" one of the fans shouted.

She?

"It's Robo Cat!"

Robo what?

"Robo Cat! Robo Cat! Robo Cat!" the crowd cheered.

"Who's Robo Cat?" asked Mom, confused.

Everyone was pointing at . . . *me?*

A fan held out her phone. There I was on the

tiny screen—riding the robotic vacuum cleaner around the television studio.

"Now Shadow is famous too!" said Cassie excitedly.

"But I don't want to be famous," I whispered to Dash. "I'll never be able to sneak outside again."

"Don't worry, Shadow," said Dash. "Fame doesn't last long." He sniffed at the air. "Plus, I think it's about to—"

Whoosh!

Rain poured down like cats and dogs. The crowd of fans scattered. We Tylers ran for the Welcome Area.

"Am I glad you're home," said Sierra, holding the front door open for us.

"Is everything okay?" asked Mom.

"Everything's fine," said Sierra. "Just one small problem. I can't find the gerbils."

EPILOGUE

I learned a lot of important

lessons from our time in the spotlight:

1. Web videos are pretty cool.

2. Limousine rides are dreamy.

3. Robotic vacuum cleaners are wild.

4. But family is what's most important.

After looking and looking, Jake and Ethan finally found the gerbils relaxing in the gerbiltorium.

"I can't believe Fuzzy and Furry were in there the whole time," said Sierra.

Ping-ping!

Sierra pulled her phone out of her pocket and tapped the screen.

"Wow," she said. "Animal Inn is just bursting with superstars."

"Yes, Super Cat is a superstar," said Dad, reaching over to pet Whiskers.

"No, not Super Cat," said Sierra.

"Oh, you mean Robo Cat," said Mom, giving me a scratch behind the ears.

"No, not Robo Cat, either," said Sierra. She held out her phone for everyone to see. "Check it out."

There on the screen was a video of Coco merrily goofing around with a small, red squirrel.

"Hey, it's Coco!" said Cassie. "And that's Curtis, the squirrel who stayed with us that time!"

I looked over at Coco. Our newest superstar was fast asleep in the middle of the Welcome Area floor.

"Remember Curtis?" said Cassie.

How could we ever forget?

FIND OUT WHAT HAPPENS IN
THE NEXT **ANIMAL INN** STORY.

Whooooo Done It?

Creak! Creak!

Rattle! Rattle!

This old house sure makes a lot of spooky sounds. There's always something creaking or rattling.

Welcome to Animal Inn. My name is Whiskers. I'm an indoor cat. I love calm, quiet, and my comfy sofa.

You might also know me as Super Cat, but that's another story.

I'm part of the Tyler family. Our family includes five humans—Mom, Dad, Jake, Ethan, and Cassie—and seven pets:

- Me
- Shadow—my big sister
- Dash—a Tibetan terrier
- Coco—a chocolate Labrador retriever
- Leopold—a scarlet macaw
- and Fuzzy and Furry—a pair of very useful gerbils

We all live together in this creaky old house in the country. Animal Inn is one part hotel, one part school, and one part spa. As our brochure says: *We promise to love your pet as much as you do.*

Squeak! Squeak!

Don't mind that. It's probably just the squeaky front door. It gets a lot of use with all the coming and going here at the inn.

We might have a Pekinese arriving for a pedicure. A Siamese showing up for a short stay. Or a llama leaving after a long stay. Once we even hosted a field trip for Cassie's entire first-grade class. That day was neither calm nor quiet. But it sure was fun.

On the first floor of Animal Inn, we have the Welcome Area, the office, the classroom, the grooming room, and the party and play room.

Our family lives on the second floor. This includes Fuzzy and Furry snug in their gerbiltorium in Jake and Ethan's room. That is, unless they're out on a case. The gerbils are excellent detectives. We pets have used their services on a number of occasions.

The third floor is for our smaller guests. We have a Reptile Room, a Rodent Room, and a Small Mammal Room. The larger guests stay out in the barn and kennels. So, at any given moment, you might hear squawks, chirps, bleats, meows, or woofs.

And just last week, we heard a sound that gave us all quite a scare and made my fur stand on end.

Promise not to get too frightened?

Okay. Let me tell you what happened. . . .

CHAPTER
1

It began on the first morning of
school vacation week.

We pets were already in the Welcome Area
when Jake and Ethan came downstairs.

I was curled up on the sofa.

Leopold was on his perch.

Dash was sitting nearby.

And Coco was plopped smack in the middle of the floor.

My big sister, Shadow, was hiding behind the sofa, waiting for her first chance to sneak outside.

"Mom and Dad said chores come first," said Jake.

"And then we can play Ghost in the Graveyard," said Ethan.

"Sounds like a plan," said Jake. He opened the door to the supply closet. "Let's see. Cat food, cat treats, dog food, dog—hold on. This is weird." Jake held up an empty bag of Doggie Donuts. "I just opened this yesterday."

"Maybe that's a different bag," said Ethan, "and the one you opened is still in there."

Jake searched the closet again. "No, I'm sure this is the bag," he said.

Jake and Ethan shrugged. Then they went ahead and filled our food bowls.

I noticed that Coco didn't budge from her spot on the floor. She kept right on snoring. She must have been really tired, because breakfast is one of Coco's favorite times of the day. Along with lunch, snack, and dinner.

Ethan returned to the closet and pulled out a broom. I should mention that brooms make me a little nervous—as do dustpans, vacuum cleaners, and leaf blowers. Too much noise and commotion.

"Whoa," said Ethan. "What happened to this thing?" He held up a feather duster—minus most of the feathers.

Before Jake could answer, Cassie appeared at the top of the stairs. She held a bright pink feather in her hand. "What happened to what?" she asked.

Jake chuckled. "I think I see what's going on here," he said. "Cassie, did you take a bunch of feathers out of the feather duster?"

"Are you and Coco putting on another play or something?" asked Ethan.

I looked down at Coco, softly snoring. She did not look like she was rehearsing for anything.

"Coco and I are not doing a play this morning," said Cassie.

"Then where did you get the pink feather?" asked Jake.

"I found it in the hallway upstairs," said Cassie.

"How did a feather from the Welcome Area feather duster get upstairs?" asked Ethan. "And where are the rest of them?"

"And the missing Doggie Donuts?" added Jake.

"How should I know?" Cassie said with a shrug.

"I thought we were going to play Ghost in the Graveyard."

"Maybe a ghost took the feathers and treats," Ethan said jokingly. "Booooo! Booooo! There it is now."

"You're just teasing," said Cassie. "Ghosts aren't real. They're just in games and stories and stuff."

"Haven't you heard about the ghost of Animal Inn?" said Jake. "On dark and windy nights, it scritches and scratches at windows and doors."

"Yeah, and whatever you do," said Ethan in a spooky voice, "don't let the ghost inside. Or Animal Inn will be haunted . . . *forever*!"

Join Zeus and his friends
as they set off on the
adventure of a lifetime.

Now Available:

#1 Zeus and the Thunderbolt of Doom
#2 Poseidon and the Sea of Fury
#3 Hades and the Helm of Darkness
#4 Hyperion and the Great Balls of Fire
#5 Typhon and the Winds of Destruction
#6 Apollo and the Battle of the Birds

#7 Ares and the Spear of Fear
#8 Cronus and the Threads of Dread
#9 Crius and the Night of Fright
#10 Hephaestus and the Island of Terror
#11 Uranus and the Bubbles of Trouble
#12 Perseus and the Monstrous Medusa

EBOOK EDITIONS ALSO AVAILABLE
From Aladdin • simonandschuster.com/kids

SHARK SCHOOL

Dive into the world of Harry Hammer in this fin-tastic chapter book series!

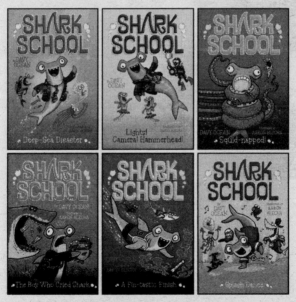

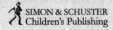